Everybody Feels...
HAPPY!

Moira Butterfield & Holly Sterling

QED

YiPPee!

Consultant: Cecilia Essau
Design: Barbi Sido, Mike Henson
Editor: Carly Madden
Editorial Director: Victoria Garrard
Art Director: Laura Roberts-Jensen
Associate Publisher: Maxime Boucknooghe
Publisher: Zeta Jones

Copyright © QED Publishing 2016

First published in the UK in 2016 by
QED Publishing
Part of The Quarto Group
The Old Brewery
6 Blundell Street
London N7 9BH

www.qed-publishing.co.uk

A catalogue record for this book is
available from the British Library.

ISBN 978 1 78493 424 8

Contents

Feeling happy!

Everybody feels happy sometimes. You might feel happy if...

...you have something exciting to look forward to.

...someone is kind to you and makes you feel good.

HAPPY!

...you do something that's lots of fun.

...you spend time with your family.

...you are kind and helpful to someone and make them feel good.

How it feels

Are you **bubbling**
with **fizzy** fun?

Is your smile really **w-i-d-e**?

Do you **feel**
full of sunshine?

That sounds gre**at**!

That sounds ...

Happy!

Happy boy

Hi, I'm Ethan. I woke up feeling very excited as **I was going on holiday!**

I was so happy I had a bubbly fizzy feeling inside, and I danced around the breakfast table.

I helped to pack my bag and I took it to
the car. I wanted to go straight away.

Let's
go!

I went on holiday with Mum and Dad and my brother Jack.

£2

YUM!

We did lots of things we'd never done before. We tried new kinds of ice cream.

We collected shells
on the beach.

We got really good on
our bodyboards, riding
on the waves.

Here I
come!

Every day was packed with things to do.

I took photos and I saved lots of tickets and leaflets from the places I visited on holiday.

When I got home I stuck them in a scrapbook.

TICKET
★★★★★

Every time I look at my scrapbook I remember the holiday we had together and I feel happy all over again!

Happy girl

Hello, I'm Sophie. I have a lot of fun with my friends, and that makes me feel happy.

One day I made two bracelets for my friend Chloe. I used her favourite colours – blue and yellow.

When she saw them she smiled and so did **I**.

Mum said she could see happiness shining from our smiley faces!

w**OW**, thanks, Sophie.

Then I thought I would pass on some more happiness.

I asked Mum if we could make some cupcakes and I gave one to my friend Omar.

Ooh. Thanks!

When my friend Ethan came round to play I lent him one of my comics.

This is **great!**

It had a story about his favourite superhero.

The next day
Chloe gave me
some bracelets
that she had made.

Omar gave me one of his mum's
delicious pastries.

Ethan gave me a pretty shell he had found on holiday.

This is for you!

My friends had passed happiness back to me!

It made me feel warm inside.

17

Happiness

Ethan felt really happy looking forward to his holiday, and he made a scrapbook so that he could remember the happy time he had.

Sophie passed on happiness by doing kind things for her friends.

Then she got it back, when her friends did thoughtful things for her.

Ethan's story

1 Ethan felt really excited on the day he went on holiday.

2 He went with his family – Mum, Dad and brother Jack.

3 He did lots of new things, which were great fun.

4 He took home some souvenirs – things that reminded him of his happy holiday time.

Sophie's story

1 Sophie made some bracelets for her friend Chloe.

2 She made a cupcake for Omar.

3 She lent a comic to Ethan.

4 Her friends returned her kindness and made her feel happy, too.

Story words

bodyboard

A short board that helps you to ride along on sea waves. Ethan used a bodyboard on his beach holiday.

collected

Picked up by someone. Ethan collected shells on the beach.

exciting

Something that makes people feel amazed and happy. Ethan's holiday was exciting.

fizzy

Full of sparkly bubbles, like a bubbly drink. Ethan thought that being excited felt like being fizzy.

ideas

Useful thoughts. Sophie had some ideas for passing on happiness.

leaflet

A folded piece of paper with information on it. Ethan collected leaflets from places he visited on holiday.

lent

When you give somebody something but you know they are going to give it back. Sophie lent Ethan a comic.

scrapbook

An empty book that you can fill with your own scraps of paper or photos. Ethan made a holiday scrapbook.

souvenir

Something you bring back from a place you visited. Ethan brought back a shell that he gave to Sophie.

thoughtful

Having a kind thought. Sophie's friends did thoughtful things for her, that they knew she would like.

ticket

A piece of paper that allows you entry to somewhere. Ethan collected some of these to put in his holiday scrapbook.

Next steps

The stories in this book have been written to give children an introduction to feeling happy through events that they are familiar with. Here are some ideas to help you explore the feelings from the story together.

Talking

- Look at Ethan and Sophie's stories. Talk about what made them happy. How did it feel to be happy?

- Discuss the things that Ethan did on holiday that made him happy. Talk about how memories made Ethan happy.
- What did Sophie do that made her friends happy? How did her friends make her feel happy?
- Ask your child to think of a time when they felt really happy, and why. Get your child to come up with some ideas for passing on happiness, like Sophie did.
- Look at the poem on page 5 and talk to your child about how they feel when they are happy. You could help them write a poem themselves.

Make up a story

On pages 20-21 the stories have been broken down into four-stage sequences. Use this as a model to work together, making a simple sequence of events about something happening to somebody that makes them happy. Ask your child to suggest the sequence of events, and be sure to include an upbeat ending.

An art session

Do a drawing session related to the feeling in this book. Here are some suggestions for drawings:

- Three or four different happy faces – so happy they are bubbling up with fizziness.
- Ethan feeling really happy on holiday.
- Chloe with her new bracelet or Omar with the cupcake Sophie made.

An acting session

Choose a scene and act it out, for example:

- Role-play Ethan on the morning of his holiday, with his family. Then act out the family on the beach, and then remembering happy things about their holiday afterwards.
- Role-play Sophie kindly giving Chloe a bracelet, Omar a cupcake and Ethan a comic. Then show Sophie's friends giving her presents back, making her feel happy.